Happy Birthday Bugs

Bugs 50th logo is a trademark of Warner Bros. Inc. © 1990

This Looney Tunes Library Book is published by Longmeadow Press
in association with Sammis Publishing.
Distributed by Book Sales, Inc., 110 Enterprise Ave.,
Secaucus, NJ 07904

With special thanks to

Guy Gilchrist • Gill Fox • Tom Brenner
Marie Gilchrist • Jim Bresnahan • Allan Mogel • Gary A. Lewis

Printed in the United States of America
0 9 8 7 6 5 4 3 2 1

BUGS BUNNY

in

HAPPY BIRTHDAY, BUGS

written by Gary A. Lewis

Illustrated by
The *Guy Gilchrist* Studios
™

ANOTHER TRUSTY
ACME PRODUCT

BUGS BUNNY
in
HAPPY BIRTHDAY, BUGS

If you had been hanging around Bugs Bunny's part of the woods one day recently, you would have seen a very strange sight.

Bugs wasn't around. (He had gone carrot shopping.) But a lot of other other familiar faces were.

They were all carrying strangely shaped packages, and all were headed for the same place. One by one, they tiptoed to Bugs' hole and then disappeared.

Inside Bugs' house, there was a whirl of activity. Stacks of brightly wrapped packages were piled on the bed. As more and more of Bugs' friends arrived, the stacks got higher and higher.

And everyone was very, very busy. Elmer Fudd and Yosemite Sam were hanging streamers. Tasmanian Devil was blowing up balloons. Porky Pig was baking a big cake.

It was Bugs' birthday, and his friends were throwing him a surprise party!

"You know," said Elmer as he worked, "I've known Bugs Bunny ever since I started in show business, and he's always been a gweat fwiend. We've had a lot of good times together."

"I know what you mean, pardner," said Yosemite Sam. "Bugs is a really dynamite critter."

"He sh-sh-sure is," added Porky, nodding.

"I wemember the time," Elmer went on, "when Bugs and I were performing together. Bugs was always so supportive. Evewy night, he would meet me at the stage door with candy and flowers."

"That boy was certainly, I say, certainly considerate," said Foghorn Leghorn.

"He's such a helpful wabbit," Elmer went on. "Did you know that he twied to cure my baldness? Unfortunately, it didn't work out vewy well. He used fertilizer instead of hair tonic. But he was weally twying to be nice."

SCOOT!

"And then there was the time when I went wabbit hunting," Elmer went on, "and I wan into Bugs and Daffy Duck. Boy, we had a wot of fun. First, they told me it was wabbit season. Then, they told me it was duck season. Then, they told me it was Elmer season! What a sense of humor Bugs has!"

Elmer scratched his head. "Although now that I think about it, Bugs had a wot more fun than I had that day."

"Bugs is certainly a character!" Yosemite Sam laughed. "He's the rootenest, tootenest hombre to ever hit the bunny trail. Why, Bugs 'n' me were pals way back. Did you know that we used to star in a carnival act together? Bugs would dive into a tiny bucket of water from all the way up above the stage. He's a brave bunny, Bugs."

"Although now that I come to think on it," Yosemite went on, "I'm not exactly sure of how it came about, but I did a fair amount of diving myself."

SLAP!

ACME BALLOONS

Yosemite smiled. "I used to land with a bang," he said. "And nobody laughed harder or applauded louder than my old pal 'n' pardner, Bugs Bunny!"

23

"Yeah, old Bugs was always a good sport," Yosemite went on. "And you probably don't know this, but he's a talented song-and-dance rabbit, too! Old Bugs and I did some singing and dancing in our act. Of course, sometimes Bugs needed a little encouragement…which I was always happy to provide."

"Although now that I come to think on it," Yosemite continued, "I used to end up doing a lot of singing and dancing myself when Bugs was around. I guess he just made me feel so knee-slappin' good!"

"Oh, yes, Bugs is a very musical bunny," Giovanni Jones, the famous tenor, agreed. "Once upon a time, Bugs actually conducted one of my concerts. I was singing my heart out, and Bugs used the baton like a true genius. I have never sung better in my entire life."

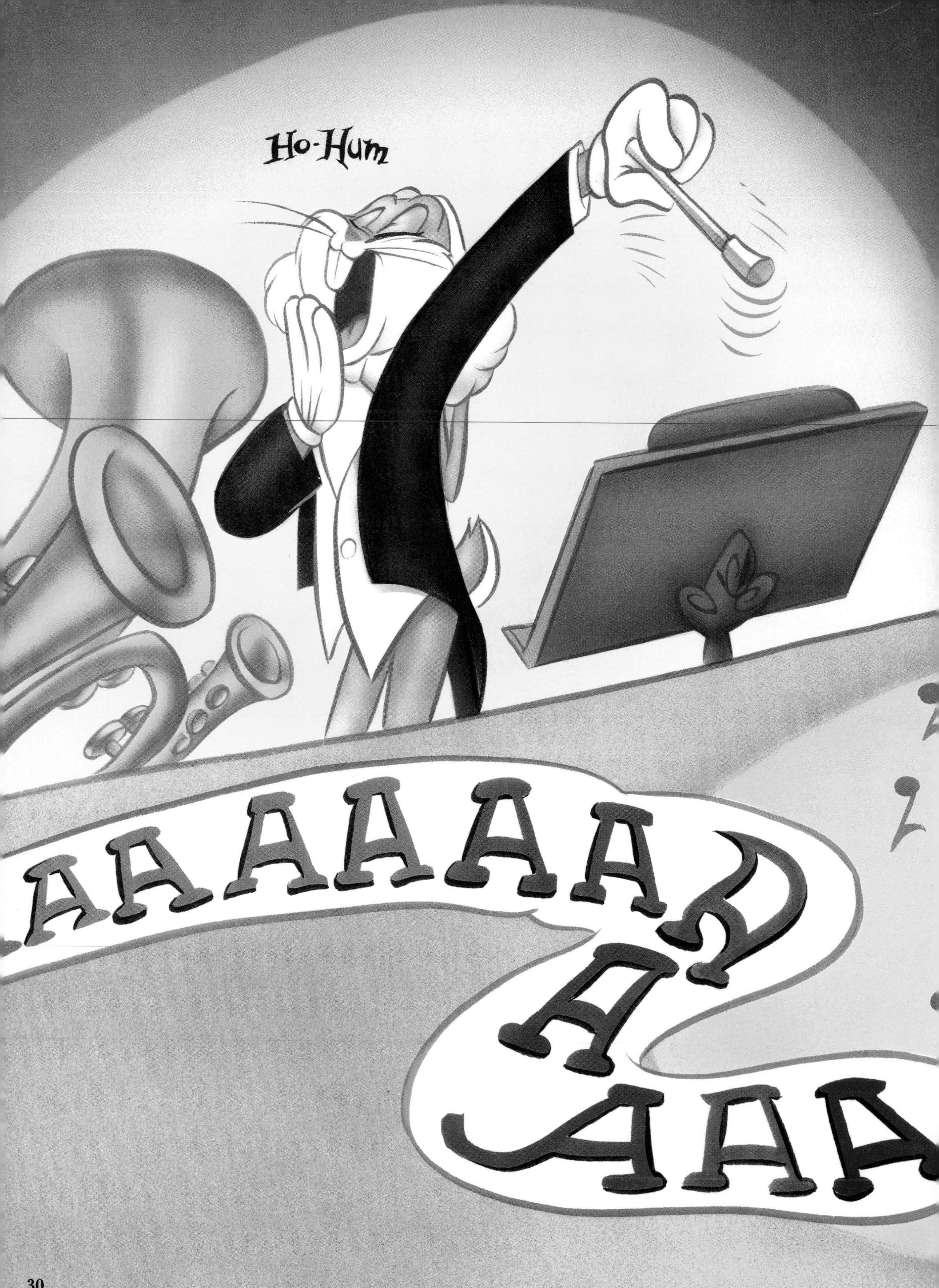
Ho-Hum
AAAAAAAAAAAAAA

"Although now that I think about it," Giovanni Jones added, "it was a very difficult program to perform. I had to sing the same high C for forty-three minutes without taking a breath. It took me a long time to recover afterwards. Working with Bugs wasn't the easiest experience of my career."

"I remember the first time I met Bugs," said Wile E. Coyote. "I was really hungry, and thinking of having rabbit for supper. So I set a trap for old Bugs."

"Oh, that bunny!" laughed Wile E., remembering. "He just stood there, munching on his carrot. He didn't even try to get away. I knew I had him!"

"But, come to think of it, something went wrong." Wile E. scratched his head. "I never did have supper that night."

"I remember the first time *I* met Bugs Bunny," said Marvin the Martian. "K-9 and I were on a special mission to Earth. Our instructions were to bring back an Earth creature to Mars for

scientific study, and the first Earth creature we ran into happened to be Bugs Bunny."

ONE OVER-
CONFIDENT
EARTH
CREATURE

"What a delightful bunny Bugs was," Marvin recalled. "He required just a little persuasion to come along with us. But after he joined us, he was so excited about the trip. Everything was just lovely."

"We took off in my spaceship, and I set the course for Mars,"
Marvin continued. "Bugs was a charming guest. He never asked for a
thing. He just sat there quietly, enjoying the scenery, keeping K-9 and
myself company."

"But now that I think about it," Marvin went on, "that Bugs Bunny played a trick on me and K-9 on the spaceship. I'm not quite sure how, but Bugs managed to untie himself and tie *us* up. Then he drove my spaceship back to Earth. And not only that…he got a speeding ticket on the way, and *I* had to pay for it!"

"I was very angry indeed," Marvin sighed.

The Tasmanian Devil blew up another balloon. "Bugs friend," he grunted. "Meet Bugs Tasmania. Bugs come visit."

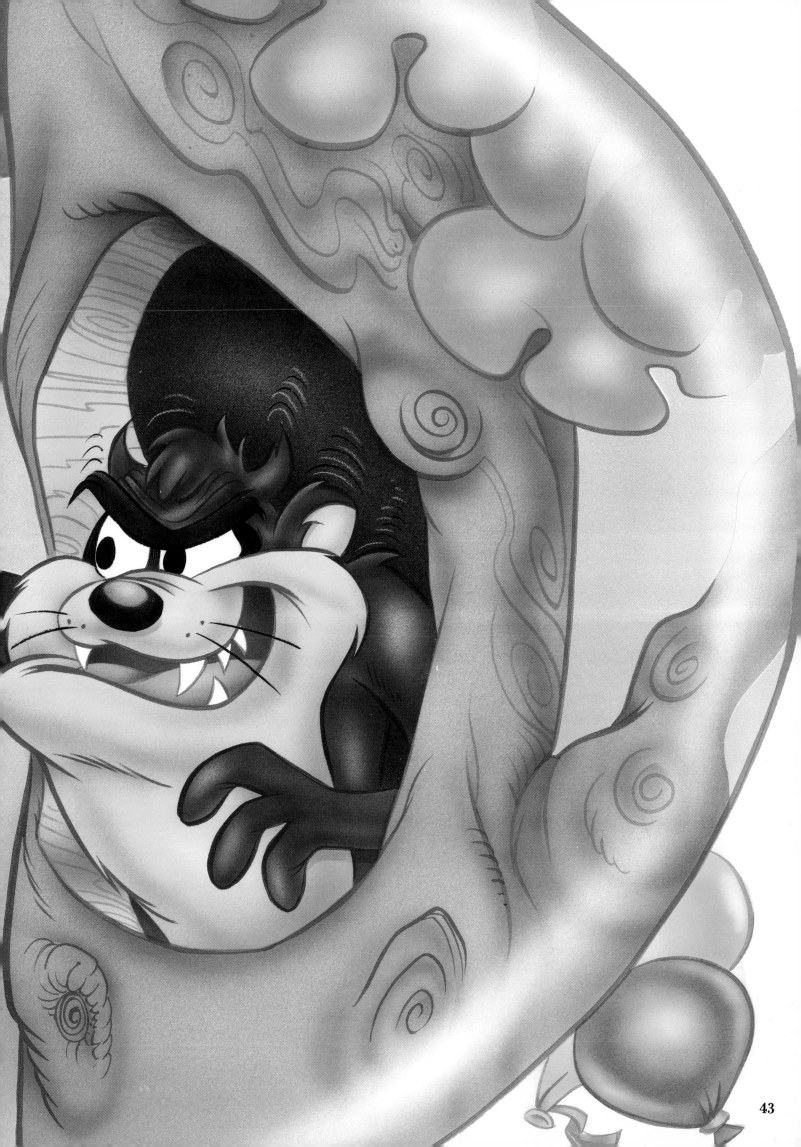

"Bugs cook meal for me," Taz went on.

"Delicious," added Taz, licking his lips. "Bugs good cook. Only one problem. Me blow up."

"You know, now that I think about it," Elmer said, scratching his head, "Bugs hasn't been the best of fwiends to any of us. He's blown us up, tied us down, pushed us off diving boards…."

"You know, you're right, pardner!" growled Yosemite Sam. "That Bugs Bunny is a rotten rabbit!"

"Y-y-you bet!" added Porky.

"So why are we giving him a surprise party?" asked Sylvester.

"I don't know," said Foghorn Leghorn. "But he doesn't, I say, doesn't deserve it nohow!"

"But since we're all here anyway," said Yosemite Sam, "I have an idea. With just a little work, we can do something to play a trick on him for a change. Let's give him a birthday present he'll never forget!"

"What do you mean?" asked Porky.
"Listen…" Yosemite began.
When he was finished, everyone laughed.
"Gweat idea!" said Elmer.
"Bugs surprise!" Taz shouted. "Surprise!"

Just as Yosemite had tied the bow on Bugs' surprise present, Tweety started hopping up and down.

"A pwetty pwesent for the bunny wabbit!" he said.

And Bugs Bunny appeared in the doorway at that very minute.

"Eh, what's up, Doc?" Bugs asked. "What are you all doing in my humble home?"

"Surprise!" shouted everyone. "Happy birthday, Bugs!"

"Aw, gee, you shouldn't have," Bugs blushed.

"Here, Bugs old pal," Yosemite Sam stepped forward. "We all did a lot of thinking about what you mean to us, and we decided to give you this little token of our esteem and affection."

Bugs took the box. "Gee, thanks, everybody," he said, shaking it. "I wonder what's inside?"

That's when Daffy showed up.

"Oh, a party for me?" he beamed. "I'm so surprised! I know how much you all love and respect me, but this is really too much."

"But th-th-this party isn't for you," said Porky.

"That's wight," Elmer added. "It's a party for Bugs. It's his birthday."

"Aw, come on," said Daffy. "Don't kid a kidder. I know a gift for me when I see it. Let me have it."

"Okay," said Bugs. "If you insist."

"I insist," said Daffy. "I insist!"

"Don't take that package!" shouted Yosemite Sam. "It's for Bugs!"

"Aw, come on!" laughed Daffy. "Why would you want to give a nice present like this to Bugs? It's obviously for me. And I want to thank

you from the bottom of my heart," he went on, "especially because I
know I deserve whatever it is."

"You said it," said Bugs.

"We warned you," Sylvester said. And everybody ducked.

Ya-Hooo!

Out of the package flew Bugs' birthday cake. It landed all over Daffy.

After Daffy had wiped the cake off his face, he sighed. "Bugs Bunny, you are dethpicable," he said. "But it's also your birthday. So…"

"Happy birthday, Bugs!" everyone yelled again. And they all agreed on one thing: Bugs Bunny's surprise party had certainly gotten off to a smashing start!